Not very o1

I'm losing weig

So do
You're welcor

May I sp

Please wrap it u

That sounds great.

Please look

Come along.

英語會話
重練更易學

ur breakfast?

Let's have a chat.

Don't smoke!

No problem.

e, please.

That's all right.

Sleep well

ve so.

ike the blue one.

With pleasure.

ow do you do?

How is your family?

get it done.

ee you.

前 言

這是一本由 ABC 學起的初級英語會話書，供未接觸過英語或者學過英語但荒疏多年的讀者使用。

成年人學英語和小孩子學英語，在方法上總會有些不同。小孩子由於智慧所限，學英語只能從單字入手，經過一段較長的時間積累，才能成功。但是成年人就不同了，因為有許許多多的生活經驗，理解力強，可以不經過正規的學習課程而掌握一種語言工具；另一方面，他們受到許多客觀條件限制，譬如在學習時間方面，就不可能像小孩子那樣充裕，也缺乏有規律的、正常的學習環境。因此，學習材料一定要切合實用，才容易記憶。學單字雖然重要，但有時候對解決實際問題並不如會話那樣有用。學會話，可以今天學一句，明天馬上派上用場；需要哪方面的會話，可以把注意力集中到哪方面去。這才是活的學習方法。

本書就是為成人學習者度身打造的，書中靈活實用的會話可供大家一邊學習一邊使用，切實提高所需語言的實際應用能力。

目 錄

Part 1

Part 2 對話 Conversation

Contents

1-01

英文字母　The English Alphabets

1-01-01.mp3

英文字母	國際音標	英文字母	國際音標
A a	〔eɪ〕	N n	〔en〕
B b	〔biː〕	O o	〔əʊ〕
C c	〔siː〕	P p	〔piː〕
D d	〔diː〕	Q q	〔kjuː〕
E e	〔iː〕	R r	〔aː〕
F f	〔ef〕	S s	〔es〕
G g	〔dʒiː〕	T t	〔tiː〕
H h	〔eɪtʃ〕	U u	〔juː〕
I i	〔aɪ〕	V v	〔viː〕
J j	〔dʒeɪ〕	W w	〔'dʌbljʊ〕
K k	〔keɪ〕	X x	〔eks〕
L l	〔el〕	Y y	〔waɪ〕
M m	〔em〕	Z z	〔zed〕

國際音標 The International Phonetic Symbols

1-01-02.mp3

國際音標	例字（附注音）	
母音	Vowels and Diphthongs	
〔iː〕	see 〔siː〕	看見
〔ɪ〕	sit 〔sɪt〕	坐
〔e〕	get 〔get〕	獲得
〔æ〕	hat 〔hæt〕	帽子
〔ɑː〕	half 〔hɑːf〕	一半
〔ɒ〕	hot 〔hɒt〕	熱
〔ɔː〕	ball 〔bɔːl〕	球
〔ʊ〕	good 〔gʊd〕	好
〔uː〕	food 〔fuːd〕	食物
〔ʌ〕	cut 〔kʌt〕	割
〔ɜː〕	bird 〔bɜːd〕	鳥
〔ə〕	sister 〔sɪstə〕	姊妹

國際音標	例字（附注音）	
〔eɪ〕	pay 〔peɪ〕	支付
〔aɪ〕	time 〔taɪm〕	時間
〔aʊ〕	now 〔naʊ〕	現在
〔ɔɪ〕	boy 〔bɔɪ〕	男孩
〔əʊ〕	home 〔həʊm〕	家庭
〔ɪə〕	dear 〔dɪə〕	親愛的
〔eə〕	there 〔ðeə〕	在那裏
〔ʊə〕	sure 〔ʃʊə〕	確實
〔aɪə〕	wire 〔waɪə〕	金屬綫
〔aʊə〕	flower 〔flaʊə〕	花

子音	Consonants	
〔p〕	pen 〔pen〕	筆
〔b〕	bone 〔bəʊn〕	骨
〔t〕	tea 〔tiː〕	茶
〔d〕	dog 〔dɒg〕	狗
〔k〕	cock 〔kɒk〕	公雞
〔g〕	gall 〔gɔːl〕	膽汁

國際音標	例字（附注音）	
〔m〕	mark 〔mɑːk〕	記號
〔n〕	night 〔naɪt〕	夜
〔ŋ〕	king 〔kɪŋ〕	國王
〔l〕	let 〔let〕	讓
〔f〕	five 〔faɪv〕	五
〔v〕	vest 〔vest〕	內衣
〔θ〕	thin 〔θɪn〕	薄
〔ð〕	they 〔ðeɪ〕	他們
〔s〕	seat 〔siːt〕	座位
〔z〕	zeal 〔ziːl〕	熱心
〔ʃ〕	shock 〔ʃɒk〕	震驚
〔ʒ〕	rouge 〔ruːʒ〕	胭脂
〔r〕	read 〔riːd〕	讀
〔h〕	heart 〔hɑːt〕	心臟
〔w〕	win 〔wɪn〕	得勝
〔j〕	yes 〔jes〕	是
〔tʃ〕	check 〔tʃek〕	檢查
〔dʒ〕	jet 〔dʒet〕	噴射

1-02

常用單詞　Common Words

人稱代詞 Personal Pronouns

1-02-01-01.mp3

對話 1

A: Are you from Hong Kong? ↗
你從香港來嗎？

B: Yes, I am. ↘ Are you from Hong Kong, too? ↗
是的。你也是從香港來的嗎？

A: No, I'm from Kuala Lumpur. ↘ So, are you a student? ↗
不，我從吉隆坡來的。那麼，你是學生嗎？

B: No, I am a clerk. ↘ In fact, I've been working since I was nineteen. ↘
我是一個文員。實際上，我從 19 歲就開始工作了。

1-02-01-02.mp3

對話 2

A: Do you know that girl over there? ↗
你認識那邊那個女孩嗎？

B: Yes, she is my friend, Julia. ↘
是啊，她是我的朋友朱莉亞。

A: Are you in the same company? ↗
你們在同一家公司工作嗎？

B: That's right. ↘ Would you like me to introduce her to you? ↗
沒錯。希望我介紹給你認識嗎？

A: That's wonderful! ↘ Thank you so much! ↘
太好啦！非常感謝！

對話 3

1-02-01-03.mp3

A: Hi, Peter, is this your book? ↗
嗨，彼得，這是你的書嗎？

B: Yes, it's mine. ↘ Are you interested in it, too? ↗
嗯，是我的。你也對這本書感興趣嗎？

A: Yes, I like its content, ↘ and the cover is very beautiful. ↘ Can you lend it to me? ↗
是啊，我喜歡這本書的內容，封面也很漂亮，能借給我看嗎？

B: No problem, go ahead. ↘
沒問題，儘管看吧。

對話 4

1-02-01-04.mp3

A: Good morning, Mrs. Brown. ↘
布朗太太，你早。

B: Good morning, John. ↘
約翰，早！

A: How are you this morning? ↘
今天早上好嗎？

B:　I'm very well, thank you. ↘ And how are you? ↘
　　很好，謝謝你。你呢？

A:　I'm fine, too. ↘ How's Mr. Brown? ↘
　　我也很好。布朗先生好嗎？

B:　He is fine, ↘ thank you. ↘
　　他也很好，謝謝你。

A:　Good-bye, Mrs. Brown. ↘
　　再見，布朗太太。

B:　Good-bye, John. ↘ See you tomorrow. ↘
　　再見，約翰，明天見。

我還想知道的單字　Know More Words

1-02-01-05.mp3

I	我	Her	她的
You	你	His	他的
She	她	Their	他 / 她 / 它們的
He	他	Mine	我的
We	我們	Yours	你的
You	你們	Hers	她的
They	他 / 她 / 它們	His	他的
My	我的	Ours	我們的
Your	你的	Theirs	他 / 她 / 它 / 們的

家人和朋友 Family and Friends

對話 1

1-02-02-01.mp3

A: Is this a photo of your family? ↗
這是你的全家福嗎？

B: Yes, it is. This is my mother, ↘ and this is my father. ↘
是啊，這是我的媽媽，這是我爸爸。

A: Your mother looks so kind, ↘ and your father is very cool. ↘
你媽媽看起來很慈祥，你爸爸蠻帥的。

B: Thanks! ↘
謝謝！

對話 2

1-02-02-02.mp3

A: That must be your sister over there,
what a pretty girl! ↘
那邊的那個女孩一定是你的姐姐 / 妹妹，真漂亮啊！

B: Everybody is saying that! ↘
大家都那麼説！

A: What does she do? ↘
她是做什麼的？

B: She is an engineer. ↘
她是工程師。

A: Can you introduce her to me? ↗
你能把她介紹給我認識嗎？

B: Sure. ↘
當然可以了。

對話 3

1-02-02-03.mp3

A: Do you have any brothers or sisters? ↗
你有兄弟姐妹嗎？

B: Yes, I have a brother and two sisters. ↘ What about you? ↘
是的，我有一個哥哥和兩個姐姐。你呢？

A: I am the only son in my family. ↘
我是家裏的獨生子。

B: Then, do you feel lonely sometimes? ↗
那麼，你有時候會覺得孤單吧？

A: Just OK. ↘ I often stay with my cousin. ↘
還好，我經常跟表哥在一起玩。

B: That's great. ↘
那還不錯。

對話 4

1-02-02-04.mp3

A: What's your friend's name, ↘ Tom? ↗
湯姆，你的朋友叫什麼名字？

B: His name is Bill, mum. ↘
他叫比爾，媽媽。

A: What's his last name? ↘ Is it Smith? ↗
他姓什麼？是史密夫嗎？

B: Yes. ↘ His name is Bill Smith. ↘
是的，他的名字叫做比爾‧史密夫。

A: Are you and Bill close friends, Tom? ↗
那麼湯姆，你們是很好的朋友嗎？

B: Not very close. ↘ I got to know him last month at a party. ↘
還算不上很好。我是上個月在一個派對上認識他的。

A: Oh, I see. ↘
哦，我明白了。

我還想知道的單字
Know More Words

1-02-02-05.mp3

family	家庭
father / dad, daddy	父親 / 爸爸
mother / mum, mummy	母親 / 媽媽
parents	父母（親）
brother	兄弟
sister	姐妹
husband	丈夫
wife	妻子
son	兒子
daughter	女兒
child	孩子
grandfather / grandpa	祖父
grandmother / grandma	祖母
uncle	叔叔 / 舅舅
aunt	嬸嬸 / 阿姨
cousin	堂兄弟姊妹 / 表兄弟姊妹
nephew	姪兒
niece	姪女
friend	朋友

數字 Numbers

對話 1

1-02-03-01.mp3

A: How many books are there on the desk? ↘
桌子上面有多少本書？

B: There are seven. ↘
有 7 本。

A: Are they new? ↗
它們都是新的嗎？

B: Yes, they are. ↘
是的，都是新的。

對話 2

1-02-03-02.mp3

A: Can I help you? ↗
你要點什麼？

B: I would like some tomatoes. ↘
我想買點番茄。

A: How many kilos? ↘
要多少？

B: Two kilos, please. ↘
請給我兩公斤。

A: Do you need anything else? ↗
還需要別的嗎？

B: That'll be all, thank you. How much? ↘
不用了，謝謝。多少錢？

A: Eighteen dollars. ↘
18 元。

對話 3

1-02-03-03.mp3

A: Do you have any rooms? ↗
您這裏還有房間嗎？

B: Yes, we have four single rooms and a double room. ↘
有的，還有四間單人房，一間雙人房。

A: We want the double room. ↘
我們要那間雙人房。

B: No problem. How many nights? ↘
沒問題。你們住幾個晚上？

A: Five nights. ↘
5 個晚上。

數字的讀法
How to Say the Numbers

1-02-03-04.mp3

關於數字的讀法大致可以分為以下幾種情況：

1. 年份 Years 的讀法：
   1998 讀作：nineteen, ninety eight
   2008 讀作：two thousand and eight

2. 電話號碼 Telephone numbers 的讀法：
   80432449 讀作：eight, o, four, three, two, double four, nine

3. 小數 Decimal 的讀法：
   18.31 讀作：eighteen point thirty one；
   0.43 讀作：naught point four three；

4. 算術式 Equations 的讀法：
   21+3=25 讀作：Twenty one plus three is equal to twenty-five.
   25-3=22 讀作：Twenty-five minus three is equal to twenty-two.
   4×2=8 讀作：Four times two is eight.
   9÷3=3 讀作：Nine divided by three makes three.

星期 / 月份 / 季節 Weeks/ Months/ Seasons

對話 1

1-02-04-01.mp3

A: What day is it today? ↘ Friday? ↗
今天星期幾？星期五嗎？

B: Yeah. I bet you didn't forget everything. ↘ What's the date today, ↘ do you know? ↗
是啊。我想你沒有忘記什麼事情吧。那你知道今天的日期嗎？

A: I bet it's July 5th. ↘ Oh, my god. ↘ Today is my wife's birthday. ↘
我想是 7 月 5 日。哦，天哪，今天是我太太的生日。

B: Luckily you remember that. ↘ Or you are bound to die. ↘
幸好你還記得。不然你就死定了。

對話 2

1-02-04-02.mp3

A: Is it Friday tomorrow? ↗
明天是星期五嗎？

B: No, it's Saturday. ↘
不，明天是星期六。

A: Really? ↗ What do you do for relaxation? ↘
　　真的嗎？那你明天打算怎麼消遣？

B: I'm going to visit my grandparents. ↘
　　我要去探望我的祖父母。

對話 3

1-02-04-03.mp3

A: Which season do you like best? ↘
　　你最喜歡什麼季節？

B: I like summer best. ↘ Know why? I like swimming very
　　much. ↘ How about you? ↘
　　我最喜歡夏天。知道為什麼嗎？因為我非常喜歡游泳。你呢？

A: Me? I like winter best. ↘ My hometown is in the north of
　　America, ↘ and there is a lot of snow in the winter. ↘ I like
　　snow very much. ↘
　　我嗎？我最喜歡冬天。我的家鄉在美國的北部，每年冬天都會
　　下很多雪。我非常喜歡雪。

B: I've never seen snow. ↘ That must be wonderful. ↘
　　我還從來沒有見過雪呢。一定很壯觀。

A: Sure. ↘
　　那當然啦。

我還想知道的單字
Know More Words

1-02-04-04.mp3

January	一月	Monday	星期一
February	二月	Tuesday	星期二
March	三月	Wednesday	星期三
April	四月	Thursday	星期四
May	五月	Friday	星期五
June	六月	Saturday	星期六
July	七月	Sunday	星期日
August	八月	Spring	春天
September	九月	Summer	夏天
October	十月	Autumn	秋天
November	十一月	Winter	冬天
December	十二月		

顏色 Colours

對話 1

1-02-05-01.mp3

A: What's your favourite colour? ↘
你最喜歡什麼顏色？

B: Purple. ↘ Most of my dresses are purple. What about you? ↘
紫色。我的大多數裙子都是紫色的。你呢？

A: I like green best, ↘ and I like pink, too. ↘ I just now bought a pink bag. ↘ Look, it's very lovely, ↘ isn't it? ↗
我最喜歡綠色，也很喜歡粉紅色。我剛剛買了一個粉紅色的手提袋。看看，它很漂亮，對吧？

B: Wow, ↘ it's really lovely! ↘
嘩，確實很漂亮！

對話 2

1-02-05-02.mp3

A: Hi, Jim. ↘ You are dressed in blue everyday. ↘
Are you fond of blue? ↗
嗨，占。你整天都穿藍色的衣服，你很喜歡藍色嗎？

B: Yes, very much. ↘ And you? ↗
是啊，非常喜歡。你呢？

A: Ditto. ↘ But I like white the most. ↘ It looks pure. ↘
我也是。不過，我最喜歡白色，看起來很純淨。

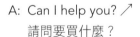

對話 3

1-02-05-03.mp3

A: Can I help you? ↗
請問要買什麼？

B: I want to buy a red bag. ↘
我想要一個紅色的袋子。

A: I'm sorry. ↘ The red ones have sold out. ↘ How about a black one? ↘
對不起，紅色的賣完了。黑色的怎麼樣？

B: Ok, thanks. ↘
好吧，謝謝。

我還想知道的單字 Know More Words

1-02-05-04.mp3

black	黑色	beige	米色
white	白色	golden	金色
yellow	黃色	silver	銀色
red	紅色	khaki	卡其色
blue	藍色	pale green	淺綠色
green	綠色	dark green	深綠色
pink	粉紅色	maroon	棗紅色
orange	橙色	blond	白皙／金黃
brown	棕色	violet	紫羅蘭色
purple	紫色		

日常用品 Appliance

對話 1

A: Are there any books on the desk? ↗
桌子上有書嗎？

B: Yes. There're three books. ↘
是的，有三本。

A: Can you pass them to me? ↘
能把這些書遞給我嗎？

B: Certainly. ↘
當然。

1-02-06-01.mp3

對話 2

A: Could you give me a hand? ↗ The door is
locked and I've no key with me. ↘
你能幫幫我嗎？門鎖上了，可是我沒帶鑰匙。

B: No problem, just give it to me. ↘
沒問題，交給我吧。

A: Thank you so much. ↘
太謝謝你了。

1-02-06-02.mp3

對話 3

1-02-06-03.mp3

A: Mum, I can't find my new watch. ↘
媽媽，我找不到我的新手錶了。

B: It's so careless of you. ↘ I put it on your desk for you. ↘
你太粗心了。我幫你把它放到桌子上了。

A: Sorry, mum. ↘
對不起，媽媽。

B: Be careful next time. ↘
下次要小心。

對話 4

1-02-06-04.mp3

A: Does anyone mind me turning on the
air-conditioner? ↗ It's hot in here. ↘
有人介意我開冷氣嗎？這裏好熱。

B: Actually, I'd prefer it if you didn't. ↘ Air-conditioners make
me sneeze. ↘
其實，我希望你不要開。因為我吹冷氣會打噴嚏。

A: All right. ↘ Would you mind me opening the window,
then? ↗ It's very stuffy in here. ↘
好吧。那麼，我開窗你介意嗎？這裏的空氣不太好。

B: Sure. ↘ That will be fine. ↘
當然可以。那樣比較好。

對話 5

1-02-06-05.mp3

A: I'm thinking about decorating my new house. ↘
I bought some books and magazines in order to
get some ideas. ↘ What do you think of this? ↘
我打算裝修我的新房子。我買了一些書和雜誌，想找些靈感。
你看怎樣？

B: They are great, especially this picture. ↘ You can fit the bed
and the wardrobe in your room. ↘
看起來不錯，尤其是這張圖片。你可以在你的房間裏放這張床
和衣櫃。

A: I also want to get the dressing table. ↘
我還想放個梳妝枱。

B: Maybe you could. ↘ If you could you'd better get a new
carpet similar to the one in the picture. ↘
大概可以。如果可以的話，你最好買張跟圖片中這個類似的新
毯子。

A: That's a good idea. ↘
好主意。

我還想知道的單字
Know More Words

1-02-06-06.mp3

window	窗戶	DVD recorder	DVD 錄影機
curtain	窗簾	washing machine	洗衣機
door	門	computer	電腦
floor	地板	humidifier	放濕機
carpet	地毯	dehumidifier	抽濕器
table	桌子	range hood	抽油煙機
chair	椅子	oven	焗爐
stool	凳子	microwave oven	微波爐
bench	長椅	induction cooker	電磁爐
sofa	沙發	rice cooker	電飯煲
bed	床	water filter	濾水器
air-conditioner	空調 / 冷氣機	dish washer	吸塵器
refrigerator	冰箱 / 雪櫃	dryer	乾衣機
television	電視	hair dryer	風筒
DVD player	DVD 播放機	heater	暖爐

食物 Food

對話 1

1-02-07-01.mp3

A: Did you have breakfast? ↗
你吃了早餐嗎？

B: Not yet. ↗
還沒有。

A: Would you like sandwiches? ↗ I made it by myself. ↘
想吃三文治嗎？我自己做的。

B: Thank you so much. ↘ It's very nice of you. ↘
真謝謝你。你太好了。

對話 2

1-02-07-02.mp3

A: What did you have for your lunch today? ↘
你今天中午吃了什麼？

B: I was too busy to have lunch. ↘
我太忙了，沒吃午餐。

A: Oh, dear me! ↘ You must be starving! ↘
哦，天哪。你一定餓壞了。

B: Exactly. ↘
就是啊。

對話 3

1-02-07-03.mp3

A: My friend asked me to dinner tonight. ↘
　朋友邀請我今天一起吃飯。

B: Do you often dine out for dinner? ↗
　你經常在外面吃嗎？

A: Yes. But I go back to my parents' for dinner on the weekends. ↘
　是的。但是我週末跟我父母一塊吃晚飯。

B: So do I. ↘
　我也是。

對話 4

1-02-07-04.mp3

A: How about having Chinese food for a change? ↗
　換換口味，我們吃中餐怎樣？

B: Great idea! ↘ I like authentic Cantonese cuisine. ↘
　好主意！我喜歡正宗的廣東菜。

A: Let's see what we can order. ↘ White stewed fish and shrimps. ↘ Anything else you want to add? ↗
　我們先想想要吃什麼。燴魚和蝦吧。你還想吃什麼？

B: Oh, yeah, beers. ↘
　哦，對了，啤酒。

A: That is it! ↘
　好，就這樣！

對話 5

1-02-07-05.mp3

A: How do you like this, honey? ↗
親愛的，你喜歡這道菜嗎？

B: How delicious! Tender and crisp! ↘
太好吃了，又嫩又脆。

A: This is the speciality of this restaurant, you know. ↘
這是這家餐館的特色菜，你知道吧。

B: Yes, it's really tasty. ↘
確實很美味。

A: I'm happy to see you enjoy it. ↘ Let's come here more often. ↘
很高興你喜歡吃。我們經常來這裏吧。

B: All right. ↘
好的。

對話 6

1-02-07-06.mp3

A: I'm starving. ↘ Let's get something to eat. ↘
我餓死了，去吃點東西吧。

B: Can we go somewhere nearby? ↗ I'm a little tired, and don't feel like walking too far. ↘
我們可以在附近吃嗎？我有點累了，不想走太遠的路。

A: All right. ↘ What kind of food do you like? ↘
好吧。你想吃什麼？

B: I'm in the mood for something spicy. ↘
我想吃辣的東西。

A: How about some Korean food? ↘ There's a place right on the corner. ↘
韓國菜怎麼樣？路口就有一家。

B: That sounds great. ↘ I love Korean food! ↘
聽起來不錯，我最喜歡吃韓國菜了！

我還想知道的單字 Know More Words

1-02-07-07.mp3

coffee	咖啡	mineral water	礦泉水
milk	牛奶	egg	蛋
yogurt	酸乳酪	beef	牛肉
bread	麵包	mutton	羊肉
cake	蛋糕	pork	豬肉
butter	牛油	chicken	雞肉
oatmeal	麥片	fish	魚肉
corn flakes	粟米片	liver	肝
juice	果汁	apple	蘋果
congee	粥	banana	香蕉
soy bean milk	豆漿	lemon	檸檬
soup	湯	orange	橙
rice	米飯	kiwi	奇異果
noodle	麵條	pear	梨
tea	茶	melon	瓜
wine	葡萄酒	water melon	西瓜
beer	啤酒	durian	榴槤

身體 Body

對話 1

1-02-08-01.mp3

A: How tall are you? ↘
你有多高？

B: My height is 180 centimeters. ↘
我身高 180 公分。

A: Do you think that you are tall enough? ↗
你覺得自己夠高嗎？

B: Yes, I'm satisfied with my height. ↘
是的，我對自己的身高很滿意。

對話 2

1-02-08-02.mp3

A: Do you like long or short hair? ↘
你喜歡長髮還是短髮？

B: I like short hair because my hair is coarse and thick. What about you? ↘
我喜歡短髮，因為我的頭髮又粗又硬。你呢？

A: I like changing my hairstyle frequently. ↘
我喜歡經常改變髮型。

對話 3

1-02-08-03.mp3

A: Did you get fat again? ↗
你又胖了嗎？

B: A little. My arms are bigger than before. ↘
胖了一點。我的手臂比以前粗了。

A: But your skin has become whiter. ↘
不過你的皮膚白了很多。

B: Really? ↗ I'm so happy to hear this. ↘
真的嗎？真高興聽到這個。

對話 4

1-02-08-04.mp3

A: It's you, Annie! ↘ How did you become just skin and bones? ↘
原來是你啊，安妮。你怎麼瘦得皮包骨啦？

B: I'm losing weight. ↘
我在減肥。

A: Why? ↘ You're not fat, ↘ and you needn't lose weight at all. ↘
為什麼？你又不胖，你根本不需要減肥。

B: You know, weight-loss is popular among most pepole. ↘
你知道，現在減肥已經是全民運動了。

A: What? ↗ Please. ↘ Health is the most important. ↘
什麼？拜託，健康才是最重要的。

B: You are right. ↘ I will exercise to keep fit. ↘
你說得對，我會做運動來健身的。

對話 5

1-02-08-05.mp3

A: Lily, I'm going to the beauty parlor. ↘
Do you want to come too? ↗
莉莉，我要去美容院。你要不要一起去？

B: Sure. ↘ Let's go. ↘ What are you going to have done? ↘
當然，我們走吧。你打算做什麼？

A: I want to have a foot massage. ↘
我想做足部按摩。

B: It sounds great. ↘ I'd also like to have a pack on my face, ↘
and get pedicures and manicures. ↘
聽起來不錯。我想做面膜，還要腳部和手部的美甲。

A: Good idea! ↘ Beauty treatments can relieve stress. ↘
好主意！美容能舒緩壓力。

B: Maybe we should try a Thai massage too. ↘
也許我們還可以試試泰式按摩。

A: What's special about a Thai massage? ↘
泰式按摩有什麼特別之處？

B: The masseuse walks on your back and massages you with her feet. ↘

女按摩師會踩在你的後背上，用她的腳給你按摩。

A: Sounds painful. ↘

聽上去好像很痛！

B: But it's comfortable! ↘

但是非常舒服！

我還想知道的單字　Know More Words

1-02-08-06.mp3

head	頭	back	背
face	臉	abdomen	腹
eye	眼睛	leg	腿
eyebrow	眉毛	thigh	大腿
nose	鼻	knee	膝蓋
mouth	口	foot	腳
tooth	牙齒	heart	心臟
tongue	舌頭	stomach	胃
lip	嘴唇	liver	肝臟
hand	手	lung	肺部
finger	手指	intestine	腸
palm	手掌	blood	血液
arm	手臂	bone	骨頭
elbow	肘部	spine	脊柱
chest	胸	muscle	肌肉
shoulder	肩		

天氣 Weather

對話 1

1-02-09-01.mp3

A: It's raining today. ↘
今天下雨了。

B: I heard that it's going to rain for the whole week. ↘
聽說這個星期都下雨。

A: What a pity! ↘ I can't go to the beach this weekend. ↘
太遺憾了！週末不能去海邊了。

對話 2

1-02-09-02.mp3

A: What a wonderful day today! ↘
今天天氣真好！

B: Yes. And it's very cool and comfortable. ↘
是啊。而且涼爽舒適。

A: I like autumn best. ↘
我最喜歡秋天了。

B: So do I. ↘
我也是。

對話 3

1-02-09-03.mp3

A: When will it clear up? ↘
什麼時候能放晴呢？

B: Maybe tomorrow. ↘
也許明天吧。

A: I don't like the cloudy and sultry weather. ↘
我不喜歡這多雲而且悶熱的天氣。

B: It's uncomfortable. ↘
確實不舒服。

對話 4

1-02-09-04.mp3

A: I went shopping without umbrella yesterday. ↘
I got caught in the rain in the afternoon.
It was raining heavily. ↘
我昨天逛街沒有帶傘。下午我被雨淋了。雨下得很大。

B: Why didn't you take umbrella? ↗
你為什麼沒有帶傘？

A: Yesterday morning was sunny. ↘ I thought the sunny spell
was going to continue. ↘
昨天早上天氣很晴朗，我以為會持續下去。

B: We really have some miserable weather here sometimes. ↘
I wish I lived somewhere which was sunny all year round. ↘
有時候我們這兒確實天氣很差勁。我真希望我住在一個全年都
陽光明媚的地方。

A: Oh, no! ↘ There would be a drought. ↘ You probably wouldn't like that either. ↘

哦，不要吧。那會太乾旱了。你可能也不喜歡。

B: I guess you're right. ↘ Maybe I just wish that the weather forecast could be more exact. ↘

我想你是對的。我只是希望天氣預報能夠更準確些。

A: The weather forecasters are not very good at prediction, ↘ because our weather is so changeable. ↘

氣象預報不能很好地預報，因為我們的天氣太善變了。

對話 5

1-02-09-05.mp3

A: How's the weather like in your city? ↘

你們城市氣候如何？

B: In the summer, it gets very hot, ↘ and it often rains. ↘ In the winter, it gets very cold and dry. ↘

夏天很熱，經常下雨。冬天很冷，很乾燥。

A: In my city, the winter temperatures usually reach about 5-15 Centigrade ↘ What are the temperatures in your city like in winter? ↘

我住的城市冬天溫度通常在 5-15 攝氏度之間。
你那裏的冬天呢？

B: Temperatures often drop below zero. ↘ It's extremely cold in
the morning, ↘ and the streets are often icy. ↘
通常溫度達到零度以下。早上非常冷，街道經常結冰。

A: Do you often have snow in winter? ↗
冬天經常下雪嗎？

B: Sometimes. ↘ Not very often. ↘
有時候會下，不過不經常下雪。

A: I've never seen snow. ↘ As you know, my city is on the coast. ↘
我從來沒見過雪。你知道，我居住的城市是海濱城市。

B: You're lucky. ↘ You can enjoy sunbathing on the beach. ↘
你很幸運，可以在沙灘上享受日光浴。

A: That's right. ↘
是的。

我還想知道的單字
Know More Words

1-02-09-06.mp3

weather report	天氣預報	drought	乾旱
sunny	晴朗	humid	潮濕
hot	炎熱	rain season	雨季
cold	寒冷	drizzle	濛濛細雨
cool	涼爽	shower	陣雨
warm	溫和	downpour	傾盆大雨
cloudy	多雲的天氣	thunderclap	雷鳴
windy	多風的天氣	lightning	閃電
breeze	微風	thunder	雷
typhoon	颱風	hail	冰雹
hurricane	颶風	fog	霧
tornado	龍捲風	mist	霧靄
frost	霜	rainbow	彩虹
snowy	下雪的	dew	露水
storm	暴風雨	flood	洪水
dry	乾燥		

交通 Traffic

對話 1

1-02-10-01.mp3

A: Do you like traveling? ↗
　　你喜歡旅遊嗎？

B: Yes, very much. ↘
　　是的，非常喜歡。

A: Do you usually travel by plane? ↗
　　你通常乘飛機旅遊嗎？

B: No. It's too expensive. ↘ I usually travel by train. ↘
　　不，那太貴了。我通常乘火車。

對話 2

1-02-10-02.mp3

A: Did you come here by bus? ↗
　　你乘巴士來的嗎？

B: No, on foot. ↘
　　不是，步行來的。

A: Really? ↗ You must be very tired. ↘
　　真的嗎？那你一定很累了。

B: Well, ↗ just fine. ↘ It's not too far. ↘
　　哦，還好。不算遠。

對話 3

1-02-10-03.mp3

A: I'll be late. ↘
我要遲到了。

B: Don't worry. ↘ You can take a taxi. ↘
別着急，你可以搭計程車。

A: But it's rush hour. ↘
但現在是繁忙時間。

B: Yes, you're right. ↘
是啊，你說得對。

對話 4

1-02-10-04.mp3

A: Excuse me. ↘ How long do I have to wait? ↘
對不起，我還要等多久？

B: I'm not sure. ↘ This is the rush hour. ↘ There's a traffic jam a few blocks away. ↗
我也不清楚。現在是繁忙時間。前面幾個街口正在塞車。

A: Let's drive off this road. ↘ I'm afraid I'll be late. ↘
我們躲開這條路吧。我擔心我會遲到。

B: It's no use. ↘ There're traffic jams everywhere this hour of the day. ↘
沒用的。這個時候到處都塞車。

A: I think we should have more roads built. ↘
我覺得我們應該多修路。

B: We have too many cars. ↘
車太多了。

我還想知道的單字 Know More Words

1-02-10-05.mp3

traffic jam	交通擁擠	highway	公路
bicycle	自行車	express highway	高速公路
car	小汽車	traffic regulation	交通規則
subway/metro	地鐵	traffic light	紅綠燈
ship	輪船	zebra stripes	斑馬線
ferry	渡輪	road junction	道路交叉點
truck	卡車	cross road	十字路
van	小型貨車	no entry	不准駛入
plane	飛機	keep in line	不准轉線
taxi	的士	no overhead	不准超越
path	小路	no turns	不准掉頭
sidewalk	人行路	parking place	泊車處
bridge	橋	a chain collision	連環撞車

1-03

常用短語　Common Phrases

對話 1

1-03-01.mp3

A: Good morning, John. ↘
　　早上好，約翰。

B: Good morning, Jane. ↘ Did you punch in yet? ↗
　　早上好，珍。上班打卡了嗎？

A: Yes , I did. ↘ What about you? ↘
　　是的，打過了。

B: Not yet. ↘ But I'll be out today. ↘
　　還沒有。不過今天我要出去。

More Phrases

Good evening. ↘	晚上好。
Good afternoon. ↘	午安。
Good night. ↘	晚安。
Good-bye. ↘	再見。
Good day. ↘	日安。
Good luck. ↘	祝你好運。

對話 2

A: Mind out! ↘ Don't touch the pot. ↘ It's hot. ↘
小心！別碰那個鍋，它很熱。

B: Don't worry. ↘ I know that. ↘
別擔心，我知道。

A: Better be careful. ↘
還是小心點兒好。

More Phrases

Be careful! ↘	小心！
Look out! ↘	小心！
Hurry up! ↘	快點！
Of course. ↘	當然。
Exactly. ↘	正是。
Quite so. ↘	確實如此。
Just so. ↘	確實如此。
Surely. ↘	的確。
Oh, I see. ↘	哦，我明白了。
That's true. ↘	那是真的。
All right. ↘	好的。
Never mind. ↘	不要緊。
Not in the least. ↘	一點也不。

對話 3

1-03-03.mp3

A: Will you attend the party tomorrow? ↗
   It will be full of fun. ↘
   你明天會參加派對嗎？會很有意思的。

B: I'm afraid I can't. ↘ I'll be very busy tomorrow. ↘
   There is a lot of work to do. ↘
   恐怕不能，我明天會很忙，還有很多工作要完成。

A: Really? ↗ What a pity! ↘
   真的嗎？那太遺憾了！

B: Yeah. If only I could join it. ↘
   是啊，要是我能參加就好了。

More Phrases

Oh dear! ↘	真可惜！	How crazy! ↘	真瘋狂！
Oh, dear me! ↘	哦，天哪！	How nice! ↘	多好啊！
What a shame! ↘	太遺憾了！	How lucky! ↘	多幸運！
Nonsense! ↘	荒唐！	Hurry up! ↘	快點！
Impossible! ↘	不可能！	By no means. ↘	決不！
How strange! ↘	真奇怪！		

對話 4

1-03-04.mp3

A: Excuse me. ↘ How can I get to the nearest hospital? ↘
請問，離這最近的醫院怎麼走？

B: Take this way. ↘ Turn right at the first crossroads. ↘
走這條路，在第一個路口向右轉。

A: Is the hospital on the right side of the road? ↗
醫院在馬路右側嗎？

B: No. It's on the left. ↘ You can see it at the crossing. ↘
不，在左側。在路口你就能看到。

A: Thank you so much. ↘
非常感謝。

B: You're welcome. ↘
不客氣。

More Phrases

Pardon me. ↘	對不起。	Thanks a lot. ↘	非常感謝。
I'm sorry. ↘	對不起。	Not at all. ↘	不客氣。
Many thanks. ↘	非常感謝。	Don't mention it. ↘	不客氣。
Much obliged. ↘	非常感謝。		

對話 5

1-03-05.mp3

A: I haven't seen you for a long time! ↘
很久沒有看到你了！

B: Yeah. ↘ I've been working in Australia last year. ↘
是啊。去年我一直在澳洲工作。

A: When did you come back? ↘
那你什麼時候回來的？

B: The day before yesterday. ↘ I'm having a party next Sunday
at my place. ↘ Will you come to my party? ↗
前天。下個週日在我家要舉辦派對。你能來參加嗎？

A: I will. ↘ Do you want me to bring anything? ↗
我會去的。需要我帶點什麼過去嗎？

B: No, just bring yourself. ↘ I hope to see you there. ↘
不用，帶上你自己就好了。希望到時候見到你。

More Phrases

Is it so? ↗	是這樣嗎？	Who? ↘ Whom? ↘	誰？
Why? ↘	為什麼？	Which one? ↘	哪個？
Why not? ↘	為什麼不呢？	When? ↘	什麼時候？
Where? ↘	在哪兒？		

1-04

常用短句　Common Sentences

命令和請求 Order and Request

1-04-01.mp3

Please be on time. ↘
請準時。

Please come in. ↘
請進。

Please come here. ↘
請過來。

Please be quiet. ↘
請安靜。

Please listen to me. ↘
請聽我說。

Please come with me. ↘
請跟我來。

Bring it to me. ↘
拿過來。

Take it out. ↘
拿出去。

Don't forget. ↘
不要忘記。

You must go! ↘
你必須去！

Don't smoke! ↘
不要吸煙！

Turn to the left. ↘
向左轉。

Wait a minute. ↘
稍等一等。

Go on. ↘
繼續吧。

Please look here. ↘
請看這裏。

Please help me. ↘
請幫幫我。

Please clean this. ↘
請把它弄乾淨。

Please spare me a few minutes. ↘
請讓我打擾你幾分鐘。

Let's have a chat. ↘
我們來談談吧。

Please remind me. ↘
請提醒我一下。

Mind your manners. ↘
注意你的舉止。

Come along. ↘
一起來吧。

Follow me! ↘
跟我來！

Do as I say. ↘
按我說的做。

Please take my word. ↘
請相信我。

Please come again next week. ↘
請下星期再來。

Come this way, please. ↘
請到這邊來。

Please wrap it up. ↘
請把它包紮起來。

Please try again. ↘
請再試試。

Let's get it done. ↘
讓我們解決它吧。

Don't be angry with me. ↘
請別生我的氣。

Pardon me for being late. ↘
請原諒我遲到。

May I speak, sir? ↗
我可以講幾句話嗎，先生？

May I have a look? ↗
我可以看看嗎？

Please give my best regards to your family. ↘
請代我向你家人問好。

Please remember me to your father. ↘
請代我向令尊致意。

Just hold the line, please. ↘
（打電話時使用）請稍等。

Don't forget to send me an E-mail often. ↘
不要忘了常給我發郵件。

Take me to the airport. ↘
請載我去機場。

Please contact me by phone. ↘
請通電話與我聯絡。

Help yourself to the soup. ↘
請自便用點湯。

Pass the salt, please. ↘
請遞給我鹽。

Come and see me when you are free. ↘
有空時來看我吧。

Let me see. ↘
讓我看看。

May I ask you for a dance? ↗
我可以請你跳舞嗎？

Please fill in this form. ↘
請填寫這個表格。

May I use your mobile phone? ↗
我可以使用你的手機嗎？

May I go home? ↗
我可以回家了嗎？

May I ask a favour of you? ↗
能幫我個忙嗎？

May I come in? ↗
我可以進來嗎？

Say it again, please. ↘
請再說一遍。

Please repeat it. ↘
請重述一次。

Please speak a little more slowly. ↘
請說得稍微慢點。

Would you please tell me where the toilet is? ↘
請告訴我洗手間在哪裏？

Would you mind changing places with me? ↗
你可以和我換個位子嗎？

Will you forgive me? ↗
你能原諒我嗎？

Will you call again later? ↗
過會兒再打過來好嗎？

Will you please show me the way? ↗
請指給我那條路好嗎？

Will you do something for me? ↗
請為我做點事好嗎？

May I trouble you for paper? ↗
麻煩你遞張報紙給我好嗎？

Would you mind shutting the window? ↗
關閉這個窗你介意嗎？

疑問和回答 Ask and Answer

1-04-02.mp3

What's this（that）? ↘
這（那）是什麼？

It's a/an ... ↘
這（那）是一個……

What's your name? ↘
你叫什麼名字？

My name is...（I'm ...）↘
我的名字叫……

What can I do for you? ↘
你想要什麼？

I'd like a glass of beer. ↘
我想要一杯啤酒。

What's the matter? ↘
怎麼了？

Nothing, I just broke a cup. ↘
沒什麼，只是我打碎了一個杯子。

What news? ↘
有什麼消息嗎？

Nothing special. ↘
沒什麼。

What are you looking for? ↘
你在找什麼？

I'm looking for my watch. ↘
我在找我的手錶。

What do you mean? ↘
你的意思怎樣？

I totally agree. ↘
我完全同意。

What happened? ↘
發生了什麼事？

I don't know. ↘
我不知道。

What do you think of that? ↘
你的意見呢？

I've no idea. ↘
我不知道。

What are you doing here? ↘
你在做什麼？

I'm cleaning the floor. ↘
我在打掃地板呢。

What's the price? ↘
多少錢？

Ten dollars. ↘
十元。

What size do you want? ↘
你要什麼尺碼？

Size 36 is OK. ↘
36 碼就可以了。

What colour do you like? ↘
你要什麼顏色的？

I like the blue one. ↘
我要那件藍色的。

May I try it on? ↘
我可以試穿嗎？

Sure, please. ↘
是的，請。

Where are you going? ↘
你要去哪？

I'm going to London. ↘
我要去倫敦。

Where did you hear that? ↘
你從哪兒聽來的？

Tom told me. ↘
湯姆告訴我的。

When will it be good for you? ↘
你什麼時候方便？

Anytime. ↘
任何時候。

When are you leaving? ↘
你什麼時候走？

Tomorrow morning. ↘
明天早上。

When will you start? ↘
你什麼時候開始？

Tonight. ↘
今晚。

Are you sure about that? ↗
你確定嗎？

Yes, I'm sure. ↘
是的，我確定。

No, I'm not sure. ↘
不，我不確定。

Are you much better now? ↗
你現在好點了嗎？

Yes, I'm better. ↘
是的，好多了。

Are you fond of fishing? ↗
你喜歡釣魚嗎？

Yes, very much. ↘
是啊，非常喜歡。

Do you speak Chinese? ↗
你會講漢語嗎？

Yes, a little. ↘
是的，會一點。

It isn't true, is it? ↗
那不是真的，對嗎？

Yes, it's true. ↘
不，是真的。

No, it's not true. ↘
沒錯，那不是真的。

2-01

招呼　Greetings

對話 1

2-01-01.mp3

A: How do you do? ↘
你好！

B: How do you do? ↘
你好！

A: My name is John White. ↘ Glad to meet you. ↘
我叫約翰‧懷特。很高興認識你。

B: I'm Julia Smith. ↘ Glad to meet you, too. ↘
我叫茱莉亞‧史密夫。見到你也很高興。

對話 2

2-01-02.mp3

A: Hi, Lily! ↘
嗨，莉莉！

B: Hi, Peter! ↘ How is everything? ↘
嗨，彼得！你最近怎麼樣？

A: Quite well, ↘ thank you. ↘ What about you? ↘
還好，謝謝。你呢？

B: Not too bad. ↘
我也不錯。

對話 3

2-01-03.mp3

A: Good morning, John! ↘
How are you going? ↘
早上好，約翰！你好嗎？

B: Hi, Lucy! ↘ I'm fine. ↘ Thanks. ↘ I haven't seen you for a long
time. How are you? ↘
嗨，露茜！我很好，謝謝。很久沒看到你了，你怎麼樣？

A: I'm very well, too. ↘
我也很好！

B: How is your family? ↘
你家人都好嗎？

A: They're all well, ↘ thank you. ↘ It's a lovely day, isn't it? ↗
他們也很好，謝謝。今天天氣真好，是吧？

B: Yes, it certainly is. ↘ How are you getting on with your French
these days? ↘
是啊，確實不錯。你近來法語學得怎樣啦？

A: Just fine, thanks. ↘
還好，謝謝！

B: That's good. ↘ Keep it up! ↘
那很好，繼續努力呀！

對話 4

2-01-04.mp3

A: Hello, Mary. Where are you going? ↘
嗨，瑪麗，你要去哪？

B: Oh, I'm just going down the street. ↘ And you? ↗
啊，我正想到街上逛逛，你呢？

A: I'm doing some shopping for my mother. ↘
我要去幫媽媽買點東西。

B: Oh, are you? ↗ How about going together? ↘
喔，是嗎？我們一塊去怎麼樣？

A: Great! ↘
太好了！

對話 5

2-01-05.mp3

A: Hi, Peter! ↘
嗨，彼得！

B: Hi, Paula! ↘ I haven't seen you for a long time! ↘
嗨，保拉！好久不見！

A: Yes , it's about two years, isn't it? ↗
是啊，差不多兩年了，對嗎？

B: Yes, I believe so. ↘
嗯，我想是的。

A: Well, how have you been? ↘
你怎麼樣？

B: Oh, pretty well, ↘ thank you. ↘ And you? ↗
哦，非常好，謝謝。你呢？

A: I've been fine. ↘ Thanks. ↘
我也很好，謝謝。

語法驛站

1. I'm 是 I am 的縮寫，其他類似的還有 he's = he is, she's = she is, we're = we are, they're=they are, haven't=have not, hasn't = has not, don't = do not, doesn't = does not 等。

2. good morning（上午用）, good afternoon（中午用）, good evening（下午用）這三句是最普通而且常用的招呼用語，無論對任何人都適合，只要時間恰當便可。此外還有 good night（晚安），用於睡覺前使用。

3. Isn't it?（不是嗎？／對不對？）是一句反問語的形式，在會話中經常用它徵詢對方意見，引起話題，並使氣氛活潑，類似的語句還有 "Is it?"（是嗎？）"Do you?"（你說是嗎？）"Don't you?"（你說不是嗎？）等等。這類反問句的用法通常是：前句如果是否定式，後句的反問語應用否定式；前句用肯定式則後句用否定式。例如：It's chilly tonight, isn't it?（今晚很冷，是不是？）It's not chilly tonight, is it?（今晚不冷，對吧？）

2-02

介紹　Introduction

對話 1

2-02-01.mp3

A: Come on, Tom, I'll introduce you to my mum. ↘
來，湯姆，我要把你介紹給我媽媽。

A: Mum, this is Tom, my classmate. ↘
媽媽，這是我的同學湯姆。

C: Hello, Tom! ↘ Peter has spoken so often of you. ↘
你好，湯姆！彼得經常説起你。

B: How do you do, Mrs. White. ↘
您好，懷特太太。

對話 2

2-02-02.mp3

A: Good morning, Mrs. Smith. ↘ May I introduce myself? ↗ I'm Janet Brown and I'm from Singapore, ↘ a friend of your daughter. ↘
早晨，史密斯太太。我可以自我介紹一下嗎？我叫珍妮特・布朗，從新加坡來的，是你女兒的朋友。

B: Is that so! ↘ I'm glad to meet you. ↘ Come in, please. ↘
是嗎！很高興認識你。請進吧！

A: Thank you. ↘
謝謝！

對話 3

2-02-03.mp3

A: Excuse me, are you Jenny? ↗
請問，你是珍妮嗎？

B: No, I'm Lucy. ↘ Jenny is in the next classroom. ↘
不，我是露茜。珍妮在隔壁的教室。

A: Thank you very much. ↘
謝謝你。

B: That's all right. ↘
不客氣。

對話 4

2-02-04.mp3

A: I believe we've met before. ↘
My name is Caroline Smith. ↘
我覺得我們好像見過面，我叫嘉露連・史密夫。

B: Yes, I remember, ↘ at Lily's party, ↘ right? ↗ I'm Jimmy. ↘
是的，我記得你，在莉莉家的派對上，對嗎？我叫占美。

A: Oh, I remember now. ↘ Very nice to see you again. ↘
對，我想起來了。很高興再次見到你。

B: Nice meeting you, too. ↘
我也很高興見到你。

對話 5

2-02-05.mp3

A: Peter, I'd like to introduce my sister Julia. ↘
Julia, this is Peter, ↘ a close friend of mine. ↘
彼得，我來介紹我妹妹茱莉亞。茱莉亞，這位是彼得，我的好朋友。

B: Hello, Peter. ↘ My brother has spoken so much of you to me. ↘
你好，彼得。我哥哥經常提起你。

C: Nice to meet you, Julia. ↘ I've been expecting to see you. ↘
見到你很高興，茱莉亞。我一直盼望着見到你呢。

語法驛站

1. 在介紹的時候，要先把男士介紹給女士；把晚輩介紹給長輩；把社會地位低的人介紹給社會地位高的人。介紹後通常會簡單的寒喧 "Glad to see you" 或者 "Happy to see you"。

2. 被介紹的時候，年輕者應待年長的先伸出手來，才可上前握手。男士也應待女士先伸出手來，這才符合西方社交習慣。

3. speak of somebody "談論起某人"。例句：

She didn't speak of her husband.
她根本沒談及她的丈夫。

They spoke of you yesterday.
昨天他們還談起你呢！

2-03

告別　Farewell

對話 1

2-03-01.mp3

A: I will have to go now. ↘
我得走啦！

B: Well, see you at school tomorrow. ↘ Drop in if you are free. ↘
哦，那明天學校裏見吧。有空來玩。

A: Yes, and don't be late tomorrow. ↘
好的，明天不要遲到哦。

B: No, I won't. ↘ See you! ↘
我不會的。再見！

A: See you! ↘
再見！

對話 2

2-03-02.mp3

A: Sorry, I have to rush off and catch the
4 o'clock plane to Singapore. ↘
對不起，我得趕緊走了，要去趕 4 點鐘去新加坡的飛機。

B: Then you must hurry up. ↘ It's 3 o'clock, and it'll take you thirty
minutes to the airport. ↘
那麼你得快點了，現在已經是 3 點鐘，去機場要用 30 分鐘呢。

A: Keep in touch then, ↘ OK? ↗
　　那麼保持聯絡，好嗎？

B: OK. ↘
　　好的！

對話 3

2-03-03.mp3

A: I'm afraid I must say good-bye. ↘
　　我恐怕得走了。

B: Why not stay a little longer? ↘
　　為什麼不多待一會兒？

A: I've got important business, ↘ and I will come again. ↘
　　我有點急事，我會再來的。

B: Soon, I hope. ↘ Well, good-bye for now. ↘
　　希望很快。那麼再見吧！

A: Good-bye. ↘ I'll be seeing you. ↘
　　再見！不久再見！

對話 4

2-03-04.mp3

A: Oh, I have to go now. ↘
　　哦，我得走了。

B: Why are you in such hurry? ↘
　　為什麼這麼着急？

A: I have another appointment at 2. ↘
我兩點鐘還有個約會。

B: Well, I won't keep you then. ↘
那麼，我不留你了。

A: See you again. ↘
再見。

B: See you. ↘
再見。

對話 5

2-03-05.mp3

A: Thanks for a wonderful time. ↘
I enjoyed it so much. ↘
謝謝你的厚待，我覺得非常開心。

B: You are welcome. ↘ We must get together again soon. ↘
別客氣。我們不久還應該再聚會。

A: Yes, we must. ↘ Well, I must go now. ↘
是啊，我們應該再聚會。好啦，我得走啦。

B: Please give my regards to you mother. ↘
請代我向你母親問候。

A: Thank you. ↘ Sweet dreams. ↘
謝謝你，願你有甜蜜的夢。

B: Sleep well. ↘
願你睡個好覺。

語法驛站

1. have to 意思為 "必須，不得不……"。它的第三人稱單數形式為 has to，過去式為 had to。在否定句和疑問句中，通常需要助動詞 do。例句：

   We have to pass the exam before we can start work.
   我們必須通過考試，才能參加工作。

   She has to stay at home every night.
   她不得不每天晚上待在家裏。

   You don't have to knock—just walk in.
   你不必敲門，直接進來就行了。

   They had to come back on foot yesterday.
   昨天他們不得不走回來。

2. I'm afraid 意思為 "我恐怕……" 通常在拒絕對方的時候，表示一種委婉的語氣。

   I'm afraid we can't come. 很抱歉，我們恐怕來不了。
   I can't help you, I'm afraid. 對不起，我幫不了你的忙。

   "Have you any milk?" " I'm afraid not."
   "你有牛奶嗎？" "對不起，沒有"。

3. why not "為什麼不……呢" 表示提出建議，有時也表示同意。例如：

   Why not go now? 為什麼不現在就走呢？

   "Let's go to the cinema." "Why not?"
   "我們去看電影好不好？" "好啊"！

2-04

請求幫助　Asking for Help

對話 1

A: Will you lend me your dictionary for a minute? ↗
　　能把你的字典借我用一下嗎？

B: With pleasure. ↘
　　可以。

2-04-01.mp3

A: Thanks. ↘ I just want to look up a word. ↘
　　謝謝，我想要查一個字。

B: Don't worry. ↘ I'm not using it now. ↘
　　不用急，我現在不用它。

A: Thank you very much. ↘
　　十分感謝。

B: Don't mention it. ↘
　　別客氣。

對話 2

A: Could you please tell me where I can buy
　　a phone card? ↘
　　請問哪裏可以買到電話卡？

2-04-02.mp3

B: You can buy phone cards in convenience stores. ↘
　　你可以到便利商店買電話卡。

A: Well, how much does a prepaid phone card cost? ↘
那麼，電話卡要多少錢？

B: The value of the prepaid phone cards varies. ↘
電話卡有各種面額。

A: OK, Thank you so much. ↘
好的。太感謝你了

B: That's all right. ↘
不客氣。

對話 3

2-04-03.mp3

A: Would you please pass me the umbrella? ↗
你能遞給我雨傘嗎？

B: Ok. But where is it? ↘
好的，但是它在哪？

A: It's there behind the door. ↘
就在門後面。

B: Oh, I see. ↘ Here you are. ↘
哦，我看到了。給你。

A: Thanks. ↘
謝謝。

對話 4

2-04-04.mp3

A: Sorry to trouble you. ↘ How can I get to the
Citibank? ↘
很抱歉打擾您。請問怎樣去花旗銀行？

B: It's not far. ↘ Cross the street and walk two blocks east. ↘
You can't miss it. ↘
不遠。穿過馬路，向東走兩個街區，你就到了。

A: Thank you very much. ↘
非常感謝。

B: You are welcome. ↘
不客氣。

對話 5

2-04-05.mp3

A: Excuse me. ↘ Is this the road to the hospital? ↗
請問這是去醫院的路嗎？

B: Yes, just go straight, ↘ at the second traffic light. ↘
The hospital is on the right. ↘
是的，只要直走就可以了，在第二個交通燈那裏。醫院在右側。

A: Thanks. ↘
謝謝！

More Sentences

2-04-06.mp3

Could you please tell me the way to... ↗
請問去……怎麼走？

How can I find... ↘
請問去……怎麼走？

Where is... ↘
請問去……怎麼走？

Turn left or turn right? ↘
向左轉還是向右轉？

Can I walk there? ↗
我可以走路過去嗎？

Where am I on this map? ↘
我在地圖上的什麼位置？

Excuse me, at which station should I get off? ↘
請問，我要在哪個站下車？

Did I take the wrong way? ↗
我走錯路了嗎？

2-05

致歉和感謝　Regrets and Thanks

對話 1

2-05-01.mp3

A: I'm so sorry to have kept you waiting so long. ↘
很抱歉讓你等了這麼久。

B: That's all right. ↘ What made you so late? ↘
沒關係,你怎麼來得這麼晚?

A: I had an emergency. ↘
我有點急事。

B: Oh, I see. ↘
哦,我明白了。

對話 2

2-05-02.mp3

A: Excuse me. ↘ May I pass, please? ↘
對不起,請讓我過去好嗎?

B: I'm sorry. ↘ I'm in the way. ↘
真抱歉,我擋住了你。

A: Pardon me, ↘ for stepping on your toes. ↘
請原諒,我踩到你的腳趾了。

B: Oh, never mind. ↘
啊,不要緊的。

A: Did I hurt you much? ↗
很痛嗎？

B: No, it doesn't hurt much. ↘
不，不怎麼痛。

對話 3

A: Did you bring my book? ↗
你把我的書帶來了嗎？

2-05-03.mp3

B: Oh, dear! ↘ I forgot again. ↘ I'm extremely sorry. ↘
哦，天哪！我又忘了。真對不起。

A: Oh, well. ↗ You'd better bring it to me tomorrow. ↘
啊，算了。明天最好帶過來。

B: I sure will. ↘
我會的。

對話 4

A: Thank you for a very pleasant afternoon. ↘
感謝你使我度過了一個十分愉快的下午。

2-05-04.mp3

B: It's very kind of you to come here and stay with us. ↘
你來和我們在一起實在太好了。

A: I enjoyed it very much. ↘
我覺得很開心。

B: So did we! ↘
我們也是如此！

對話 5

2-05-05.mp3

A: Thank you so much for your help, Mike. ↘
太感謝你的幫忙了，麥克。

B: Don't mention it. ↘ I'm glad to be able to help you. ↘
沒關係的。我很高興能幫到你。

A: Thank you. ↘
謝謝你。

B: Don't hesitate to ask when you need help. ↘
有需要我的地方請儘管提出來。

語法驛站

1. Excuse me, Pardon me 和 I'm sorry 這三句話都是表示抱歉的語句。意思分別為 "打擾了"、"請恕我失禮" 和 "對不起"。I'm sorry 還表示我 "很難過"。至於向陌生人詢問什麼事情，則用 Excuse me 或 Pardon me。

2. 別人向你表示歉意的時候，應該有容人的態度。最常用的回答是 "That's all right" 或 "It's all right"。這是最得體最有禮貌的說法。"Never mind" 只適合用於熟稔的朋友。"Forget it" 則答得比較勉強，用的時候要小心。

打電話及拜訪　Calling and Visiting

2-06-01.mp3

對話 1

A: Hello? ↗
　　喂？

B: Hello? ↗ Is this eight nine zero five two four three two? ↗
　　喂？是 89052432 號嗎？

A: No, ↘ This is eight nine zero five two four two three. ↘
　　不，這裏是 89052423 號。

B: Isn't this Mr. Brown's home? ↗
　　不是布朗家嗎？

A: No, this is a bookstore. ↘ You got the wrong number. ↘
　　不，這裏是書店。你打錯電話了。

B: I'm sorry. ↘
　　對不起。

對話 2

2-06-02.mp3

A: Hello! ↘ Whom do you want to speak to? ↘
　　你好，請問你找哪位？

B: I wish to speak to Danny. ↘
　　我想跟丹尼通話。

A: Just hold the line, please. ↘
　　請等一等。

B: Yes, thank you. ↘
　　好的，謝謝你。

對話 3

2-06-03.mp3

A: Hello? ↗
　　喂？

B: Hello? ↗ This is John speaking. ↘ Is that you, ↘ Lily? ↗
　　喂？我是約翰。是你嗎，莉莉？

A: Yes, John. ↘ It's very noisy. ↘ Can you speak louder? ↗
　　是我，約翰。我這兒很吵，能講話大點聲音嗎？

B: Yes. ↘ May I see you for a minute now? ↗
　　好的。我現在能見見你嗎？

A: Certainly. ↘ But please come over ten minutes later. ↘
　　當然可以。不過請 10 分鐘以後過來。

B: OK. See you soon! ↘
　　好的，一會兒見！

A: See you soon! ↘
　　一會兒見！

對話 4

2-06-04.mp3

A: Hello, is Mr. Black in? ↗
喂，請問布萊克先生在嗎？

B: No, he isn't in just now. ↘
不，他現在不在。

A: Oh! Is he? ↗
哦，是嗎？

B: Would you like to leave a message? ↗
可以留下口信嗎？

A: Please tell him to call Mr. Smith later. ↘
請告訴他等會兒給史密夫先生回電話。

B: Yes, I will. ↘
好的，我會的。

對話 5

2-06-05.mp3

A: Good morning. ↘ Is Dr. Brown in? ↗
早上好，布朗博士在嗎？

B: Yes, he is. May I ask your name? ↗
是的，他在。請問你貴姓？

A: I'm John Smith, his student. ↘ I'd like to see him. ↘
我是約翰·史密夫，他的學生。我想見見他。

B: All right. ↘ Wait a moment. ↘ I'll call him. ↘
好的，請等一等。我去叫他。

A: Thanks. ↘
謝謝。

對話 6

2-06-06.mp3

A: Good evening! ↘
晚上好！

B: Good evening! ↘ It's nice to see you, Joseph. ↘
晚上好！很高興見到你，約瑟。

A: Is Bob at home? ↗
卜在家嗎？

B: I'm sorry. ↘ He went out for a walk. ↘
不好意思，他出去散步了。

A: Will he be back right away? ↗
他會很快回來嗎？

B: I think he'll be back soon. ↘
Can't you come in for a while? ↗
我想他一會兒就回來了。進來坐一會兒好嗎？

A: Well, won't I be disturbing you? ↗
好的，我不會打擾你吧？

B: No, not at all. ↘
不，哪兒的話。

語法驛站

1. 打電話時，不說 "I am..." "are you...?" 而是說 "This is ..." "Is that...?". 例如：This is Bob speaking. Is Tom in? 我是卜。湯姆在家嗎？

2. Somebody is in. 意思是 "某人在家"。

   He is not in.
   他不在家。

2-07

希冀和願望　Hope and Wish

對話 1

2-07-01.mp3

A: What would you like to eat? ↘
你想吃什麼？

B: I don't know much about this restaurant. ↘
我對這家餐廳不熟。

A: What about some sashimi and sushi? ↘
魚生和壽司怎麼樣？

B: That must be wonderful. ↘
一定很好吃。

對話 2

2-07-02.mp3

A: I wish to see your manager. ↘
我想見你們的經理。

B: Have you made an appointment with him? ↗
你和他約好了嗎？

A: Yes. ↘
是的。

B: Wait a moment, please. ↘
請稍等。

A: Thank you. ↘
謝謝。

對話 3

2-07-03.mp3

A: I wish I could have a long holiday! ↘
我希望我能有個長假！

B: Where are you going then if you had? ↘
如果你有的話，你要去哪裏？

A: I'd love to go to the Europe. ↘
我想去歐洲。

A: Marvelous! ↘ I'm longing for that, too! ↘
那簡直太棒了！我也希望呢！

對話 4

2-07-04.mp3

A: Why do you fix your eyes on the bike? ↘
你為什麼盯着那輛自行車？

B: If only I could have it! ↘
要是我能擁有該多好！

A: You will have it on your birthday. ↘
到你生日那天你會有的。

B: Why not now, ↘ Mum? ↗
為什麼不現在買，媽媽？

對話 5

2-07-05.mp3

A: I'd like to drop drawing. ↘
我想要放棄畫畫。

B: Why? ↘
為什麼？

A: I'm too busy learning English and Maths. ↘
我太忙了，要學習英語和數學。

B: What a pity! ↘
真是太遺憾了！

More Sentences

2-07-06.mp3

I am looking forward to... ↘
我期待着……

I'd love to... ↘
我期望……

I can't wait for... ↘
我等不及要……

I'm dying for... ↘
我期待……

I'd rather... ↘
我想要……

I'm hoping that... ↘
我希望……

I feel like... ↘
我喜歡……

2-08

喜歡和厭惡　Like and Dislike

2-08-01.mp3

對話 1

A: Do you like pop music? ↗
你喜歡流行音樂嗎？

B: No, I like classical music better. ↘
不，我更喜歡古典音樂。

A: It has unfailing charm, doesn't it? ↗
古典音樂有永恆的魅力，是吧？

B: Yes, it does. ↘
是啊，確實如此。

2-08-02.mp3

對話 2

A: Do you like dancing? ↗
你喜歡跳舞嗎？

B: No, I'm not good at that. ↘
I like sports, especially badminton. ↘
不，我不擅長跳舞。我喜歡運動，尤其是打羽毛球。

A: Really? ↗ I like badminton, too! ↘ Would you like to play badminton with me this weekend? ↗
真的嗎？我也喜歡打羽毛球！這個週末你願意跟我一起去打羽毛球嗎？

B: OK, let's make it on Sunday afternoon. ↘
好啊，就定在週日下午吧。

對話 3

2-08-03.mp3

A: I really enjoy cooking. ↘
我很喜歡烹飪。

B: What do you like to cook? ↘
你喜歡做什麼？

A: I like baking in my spare time. ↘
我一有空閒就喜歡烘焙。

B: Wow, the desserts must be delicious. ↘ But I'm afraid of putting on weight. ↘
嘩，那些點心一定很好吃。不過我很擔心發胖。

對話 4

2-08-04.mp3

A: How do you like this film? ↘
你喜歡這部電影嗎？

B: Personally I don't like it. ↘
我個人不喜歡。

A: Why not? Don't you think it's very exciting? ↗
為什麼不喜歡呢？你不覺得很刺激嗎？

B: I think it's frightening! I'm scared! ↘
我覺得很嚇人！我怕得不得了！

2-08-05.mp3

對話 5

A: Don't mention him around me. ↘
別在我面前提到他。

B: Why？↘
為什麼？

A: I can't bear his attitude. ↘
我無法忍受他的態度。

B: Can't you try to accept him? ↘
你就不能試着接受他嗎？

A: Don't even think about it! ↘
想都別想！

B: Oh, I'm so disappointed. ↘
哦，我可真失望。

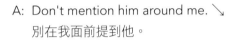

More Sentences

2-08-06.mp3

我喜歡……	我不喜歡……
I love... ↘	I don't care for... ↘
I'm keen on... ↘	I can't stand... ↘
What's your favourite? ↘	I don't like... ↘
I would like... ↘	I hate... ↘
There's nothing I enjoy more than... ↘	I don't think highly of... ↘

2-09

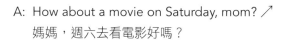

家居生活　Daily Life

對話 1

2-09-01.mp3

A: How about a movie on Saturday, mom? ↗
媽媽，週六去看電影好嗎？

B: Well, I'm afraid not Saturday, baby. ↘ I'll be too busy that day. ↘ How about Sunday? ↘
嗯，週六恐怕不行，寶貝。那天我會很忙。星期天怎樣？

A: That sounds fine. ↘
也不錯。

對話 2

2-09-02.mp3

A: Tom, could you do me a favor? ↗
湯姆，能幫我個忙嗎？

B: What's up, mum? ↗
什麼事，媽媽？

A: We don't have much salt. ↘ Can you buy some? ↗
家裏沒有足夠的鹽了，你能去買些回來嗎？

B: Sure, in a minute. ↘
好的，馬上就去。

A: By the way, buy some vinegar. ↘
順便買點醋吧。

對話 3

2-09-03.mp3

A: How do you like TV series? ↘
你喜歡看電視連續劇嗎？

B: Personally I don't like them. ↘ I think it's a waste of time. ↘
But I like variety shows. ↘
我不怎麼喜歡。我覺得那就是浪費時間。不過我喜歡綜藝節目。

A: Me, too. ↘ I like the host with sense of humor. ↘
我也是，我喜歡幽默的主持人。

B: Yes, I agree. ↘
是啊，我也是。

對話 4

2-09-04.mp3

A: Hurry up, Lucy! ↘ We're all waiting for you. ↘
快點，露茜！我們都在等你。

B: Just a minute. ↘ I'm coming. ↘
馬上，我來了。

A: I hope we won't be late. ↘
但願我們不會遲到。

B: It's early. Don't worry. We won't be late. ↘
還早呢，別擔心。我們不會遲到的。

A: I hope so. ↘
但願如此。

語法驛站

1. How about = What about 表示"……怎麼樣？"是口語中很常用的表達方式，尤其在向對方提出建議的時候，譬如：

   How about going for a walk? 去散散步好嗎？

   How about a hot bath? 洗個熱水澡怎麼樣？

2. By the way 意思是"順便說一句，除此之外，順便一提"。通常用在從一個話題轉移到另外一個話題的時候。如果談到某個令人尷尬的話題時，就可以用這個句子來改變談話的氣氛。例句：

   By the way, do you live with your parents or have a place of your own?
   順便問一句，你是跟父母一塊生活還是自己生活？

   By the way, what happened to that girl at last?
   順便問一下，那個女孩後來怎麼了？

3. I hope... 表示"我希望……；但願……"例句：

   I hope you're well. 希望你健康。

   We hope you will be here earlier tomorrow.
   我們希望你明天能早點來這裏。

   I hope so. 但願如此。

2-10

減肥和健康　Diet and Health

對話 1

2-10-01.mp3

A: Hey! ↘ You look really fresh today! ↘
嗨！你今天看起來真精神！

B: Thanks. ↘ Perhaps it's because I've lost weight successfully. ↘
謝謝！大概是因為我減肥成功了吧。

A: How many pounds have you lost? ↘
你瘦了幾磅？

B: About eight pounds. ↘
大約 8 磅。

A: Great! ↘ Don't do your health harm while losing weight. ↘
太好了。減肥可別傷害了身體哦。

B: Thanks. ↘ I won't. ↘
謝謝，我不會的。

對話 2

2-10-02.mp3

A: It's too expensive to go to a fitness center. ↘
去健身中心減肥太貴了。

B: Lose weight? ↗ Why bother! ↘ You are not fat. ↘
減肥？為什麼減肥？你又不胖。

A: I think there's enough room for me to lose a little weight. ↘
我覺得自己還可以再瘦點。

B: It's not good to be too thin. ↘
太瘦了並不好。

A: Well, I hope my weight will drop to 110 pounds. ↘
嗯，我希望我的體重能降到 110 磅。

B: Good luck. ↘
祝你好運！

對話 3

2-10-03.mp3

A: Are you still taking the slim pills? ↗
你還在吃減肥藥嗎？

B: No. I've stopped taking them. ↘ I do exercise every morning instead. ↘
沒有，我已經不吃了。我現在每天早上鍛鍊身體。

A: How is it going on? ↘
怎麼樣？

B: I feel wonderful. ↘
我覺得好極了。

對話 4

2-10-04.mp3

A: Do you still stay up often? ↗
你仍然經常熬夜嗎？

B: I'm trying my best to avoid that. ↘
我正在盡量避免。

A: You're right. ↘ You'd better keep your lifestyle in a more regular pattern. ↘
這樣就對了。你最好讓生活變得更加有規律點。

B: I will. ↘
我會的。

對話 5

2-10-05.mp3

A: You look rather pale. ↘
你看起來臉色蒼白。

B: I felt dizzy when I got up this morning. ↘
今天早上起來我就覺得頭暈。

A: Did you have fever last night? ↗
你昨晚有發燒嗎？

B: I can't tell exactly, but I didn't sleep well. ↘
我也說不清楚，但是睡得不好。

A: You'd better see your doctor immediately. ↘ I think. ↘
我想，你最好快點去看醫生。

B: Yes, I'll take your advice. ↘
好的，我會聽你的勸告。

對話 6

2-10-06.mp3

A: You don't look well, ↘ is there anything wrong? ↗
你的臉色看起來不大好，有什麼不舒服嗎？

B: Yes, I have a stomachache. ↘
是的，我的胃痛。

A: You must lie down for a while. ↘
你應該躺一躺。

B: All right, thank you. ↘
好的，謝謝你。

A: Shall I call a doctor? ↗
我去請醫生好嗎？

B: No, I think I'll be all right in a minute. ↘
不必了，我想我會很快好的。

對話 7

2-10-07.mp3

A: Hi, Jojo. You look not well. How are you feeling? ↘
嗨，祖祖！你看起來臉色不好，感覺怎麼樣？

B: I am not feeling so well. ↘
我感覺不舒服。

A: Did you see a doctor? ↗
　　去看過醫生了嗎？

B: Yes, I just came back from the doctor. ↘
　　是的，我剛剛從醫生那兒回來。

A: You should take care of yourself. Health is a man's best wealth. ↘
　　你要注意身體啊。健康是人最大的財富。

B: I know. I will take care. ↘ Thank you. ↘
　　我知道，我會當心的。謝謝你。

語法驛站

1. look 表示"看起來"，後面直接加形容詞表示"看起來怎麼樣"。例如：

look fine 看起來臉色不錯

look uncomfortable 看起來不舒服

don't look well 看起來不太好

look nice 看起來很漂亮等等。

當主語是第三人稱單數的時候，look 要用 looks 的形式，例如：

He looks very well
他看起來非常健康。

語法驛站

2. harm，意思為傷害。

do somebody/something harm=do harm to somebody/
something 表示對某人 / 某事物有害。例句：

Getting up early does no harm to you (Getting up early
won't harm you)！
早起對你沒有壞處！

mean no harm 意為"沒有惡意"。例句：

I mean no harm to her.
我對她並無惡意。

He means no harm to you.
他對你並無惡意。

3. You'd better 是 You had better 的縮寫。

Had better 的意思是"最好……"例句：

We had better go before the rainstorm becomes worse.
我們最好趕在暴雨更大以前走。

You'd better not invite him.
你最好不要邀請他。

We'd better stay here.
我們最好留在這裏。

2-11

健身和美容　Fitness and Beauty

對話 1

2-11-01.mp3

A: I really think a little exercise would do you good. ↘
Why don't you join a fitness center? ↘
我真的覺得做運動對你有好處。你為什麼不去報名參加健身俱樂部呢？

B: But I think walking up and down the stairs would beat any exercise machine. ↘
但是我覺得上落樓梯比任何健身設備都好。

A: Maybe you're right. ↘
也許你説得對。

對話 2

2-11-02.mp3

A: I really need to work out. ↘
我真的需要鍛鍊身體了。

B: Why don't you attend an aerobic class? ↘
你為什麼不參加一個有氧運動班呢？

A: An aerobic class? ↗ It sounds good. ↘
有氧運動班？聽起來不錯啊。

B: Combining exercise with the diet may be the most effective way to lose weight. ↘
運動和節食結合也許是減肥最有效的途徑。

A: That's right. ↘
說得沒錯。

對話 3

2-11-03.mp3

A: You look full of energy! ↘ How do you make it? ↘
你看起來精力充沛，怎麼做到的？

B: Jogging. ↘ I find jogging does me good, so I keep on doing it. ↘
慢跑。我發現慢跑對我身體很有好處，所以我就堅持下來了。

A: Really? ↗ I'd better exercise my body too. ↘
真的嗎？我也應該鍛鍊身體了。

對話 4

2-11-04.mp3

A: Do you trust those beauty masks? ↗
你相信面膜的功效嗎？

B: Certainly. ↘ I'm a lover of beauty masks. ↘
當然了。我非常喜歡面膜。

A: No wonder you looked so pretty! ↘
難怪你看起來這麼漂亮！

B: Don't flatter me again. ↘ But it seems that the sentence is right. ↘
There're no ugly women, just lazy ones. ↘
別再灌我迷魂湯了。不過看來那句話是對的。沒有醜女人，只有懶女人。

More Sentences

2-11-05.mp3

我需要……

I need to... ↘

I have to... ↘

I should... ↘

I'd better... ↘

充滿……

I'm full of energy. ↘

我充滿了活力。

The bottle is full of water. ↘

瓶子裏裝滿了水。

His mind is full of surprising ideas. ↘

他滿腦子都是令人驚奇的點子。

2-12

飲食　Food and Beverage

對話 1

A: Which do you like better, apples or oranges?
蘋果和橙你更喜歡哪個？

2-12-01.mp3

B: I like apples better.
我更喜歡蘋果。

A: Why?
為什麼？

B: Because apples are much more tasty.
因為蘋果更合我的口味。

對話 2

A: What would you like, coffee or tea?
你要喝咖啡還是茶？

2-12-02.mp3

B: Coffee, please.
咖啡。

A: Black coffee or three-in-one?
黑咖啡還是三合一咖啡？

B: I drink my coffee black. What about you?
我喜歡黑咖啡。你呢？

A: Tea is my favourite. ↘
我最喜歡喝茶。

對話 3

2-12-03.mp3

A: Please sit over here. ↘
What will you have to drink? ↘
請坐到這邊來。請問你想喝點什麼呢？

B: Nothing, thanks. ↘ I don't drink. ↘
不必了，謝謝。我是不喝酒的。

A: What about a beer, then? ↗
那麼，啤酒如何？

B: Not even beer, thanks. ↘
啤酒也不必了，謝謝。

A: I hope you'll like the soup. ↘
我希望你會喜歡這種湯。

B: Yes, it's excellent. ↘
是的，這個湯妙極了！

對話 4

2-12-04.mp3

A: Won't you have any more? ↗
你可再添一些嗎？

B: I think I will. ↘ It's delicious. ↘
我想再要些。它很可口。

A: Help yourself to the soup. ↘
請再喝點湯吧。

B: I've had quite enough. ↘ Thank you. ↘
我已經很飽了，謝謝。

A: Here are fruits in season. ↘ Try the grapes. ↘
這裏有時令水果，吃點葡萄。

B: Oh! How sweet they are! ↘
啊，真甜！

2-12-05.mp3

對話 5

A: Which restaurant do you prefer? ↘
你想去哪家餐館？

B: I'd like to have seafood for a change. ↘
我想換換口味，吃海鮮吧。

A: Great idea! ↘ What about sea cucumber and lobster? ↘
好主意！吃海參和龍蝦怎麼樣？

B: I totally agree! ↘
完全同意！

A: Why not go now? ↘
為什麼不現在去呢？

B: Let's go! ↘
我們走吧！

語法驛站

1. 詢問對方想吃什麼的時候，最常用的句式就是："What would you like?"，回答通常是"I'd like..."。例句：

   "What would you like for dinner, John?" "I'd like noodles."
   "約翰，你晚上想吃什麼？" "我想吃麵條。"

   "What would you like for your breakfast?" "I'd like bread and milk."
   "你早餐想吃什麼？" "我吃麵包和牛奶。"

2. Great idea! 好主意！表示非常贊同對方。也可以說 "Good idea!" "Splendid idea!"。
   例句：

   "Why don't we take a holiday in Hawaii" "Great idea!"
   "我們去夏威夷度假好不好？" "真是好主意！"

2-13

週末和節日　Weekends and Festivals

對話 1

2-13-01.mp3

A: Jane, what will you do this weekend? ↘
珍妮，你這個週末要做什麼？

B: I'll go to the beach with Peter. ↘
But it depends on the weather. ↘
我要和彼得去海邊。但是得看天氣情況。

A: Yes, exactly. ↘ You'd better listen to the weather forecast. ↘
沒錯。你最好聽聽天氣預報。

對話 2

2-13-02.mp3

A: Will you go out with us this Saturday? ↗
你願意這個週六跟我們一起郊遊嗎？

B: I'm afraid I can't. ↘ I want to have a complete relaxation this
weekend. ↘
恐怕不行。我想這個週末徹底休息。

A: If only you could join it! ↘
如果你能來就好了！

B: Maybe next time. ↘ Enjoy your time! ↘
下次吧。祝你們玩得愉快！

對話 3

2-13-03.mp3

A: Sophie, how was your weekend? ↘
索菲，你這個週末過得怎樣？

B: Really good! ↘ I went hiking in the mountains with my friends on Sunday. ↘
非常好！我跟朋友週日去遠足了。

A: Fantastic! ↘ How was that? ↘
真棒！遠足感覺怎樣？

B: Great! ↘ You should try it sometime. ↘ But I am still tired now. ↘
太好了。哪天你也應該試試。不過我到現在還累呢。

對話 4

2-13-04.mp3

A: How do you plan to spend Christmas holidays this year? ↘
今年的聖誕節你打算怎麼過？

B: With my family, I suppose. ↘ What about you? ↘
我想跟家人在一起。你呢？

A: I'll be on a tour to Europe. ↘
我會去旅行，去歐洲。

B: That's great. ↘ What do you want to see particularly? ↘
真好。你特別想去哪兒？

A: The alps. ↘ You know, I like skiing. ↘
阿爾卑斯山。你知道，我喜歡滑雪。

B: Yes, that's a wonderful place for you. ↘ I hope I'll have a chance to visit. ↘
是啊，那確實是個非常適合你的地方。我希望我也有機會去。

A: You will. ↘
你也會有機會的。

對話 5

2-13-05.mp3

A: How many official days off for Labor Day in Hong Kong? ↘
在香港勞動節的法定假期有幾天？

B: One day. ↘
一天。

A: What a pity! ↗
真可惜！

B: Yes, only one Day! ↘
對，只有一天。

More Sentences

2-13-06.mp3

……（時間）你打算做什麼？

What will you do...? ↘

What's your plan...? ↘

What do you want to do...? ↘

How will you spend...? ↘

你知道這些假日怎麼說嗎？

Christmas	聖誕節
Lunar New Year's day	農曆新年
Saint Valentine's Day	情人節
Ching Ming Festival	清明節
Tuen Ng Festival	端午節
Chinese Mid-Autumn Festival	中秋節
Chung Yeung Festival	重陽節
National Day	國慶節

2-14

旅遊　Travel

對話 1

2-14-01.mp3

A: Have you ever been to any other country? ↗
你去過別的國家嗎？

B: Yes, I've travelled many countries. ↘
是的，我曾經旅行過很多國家。

A: Can you suggest anywhere? ↗
能推薦一下嗎？

B: Greece. ↘ I like it the best. ↘
希臘。我最喜歡那裏。

A: If I can afford it, I certainly take a trip there. ↘
如果我有錢的話，我一定去那旅行。

B: Sure. ↘ It's a beautiful place. ↘
沒錯。那是個漂亮的地方。

對話 2

2-14-02.mp3

A: Did you have a good trip? ↗
你旅行愉快嗎？

B: Sure. ↘ I visited the Great Wall. ↘ It's really great and I like the sight very much. ↘
當然。我去了長城。真的很壯觀，我非常喜歡那兒的景色。

A: Did you go there alone? ↗
你是自己去的嗎？

B: No, it's a package tour. ↘ I didn't have to worry about accommodation, meals or those sort of things. ↘
不是，是跟團旅行。我不想費心思安排住宿和膳食那樣的事情。

A: You are right. ↘
說得沒錯。

對話 3

2-14-03.mp3

A: Can you think of anywhere I could go? ↗
你能推薦給我玩的地方嗎？

B: We have a beautiful natural park in the east of the city. ↘
城東有一個很漂亮的自然公園。

A: Thank you. ↘ I'd like to buy some souvenirs. ↘ What's this city famous for? ↘
謝謝。我還想買些紀念品。這裏什麼東西出名？

B: Nothing special. ↘
沒什麼特別的。

A: Thank you all the same. ↘
不管怎麼說，謝謝你。

對話 4

2-14-04.mp3

A: How often do you fix up trips every year? ↘
你每年安排幾次旅行？

B: That depends. ↘ I usually go abroad for tourism every year. ↘
不一定。我通常每年出國旅行一次。

A: Do you prefer going with a group or going on your own? ↘
你喜歡跟團旅行還是自助旅行？

B: I like to be on my own. ↘
我喜歡自助遊。

A: Why? Isn't it dangerous? ↘
為什麼？不危險嗎？

B: Not at all. ↘ It's full of fun. ↘
一點也不。自助遊充滿了趣味。

A: I'd like to try next time! ↘
下次我也要試試！

B: You'll enjoy it! ↘
你會很喜歡的！

語法驛站

1. Have you been to... 表示 "你曾經去過……嗎" ？例句：

    "Have you been to Canada?" "Yes, I've been there
    several times"
    "你去過加拿大嗎？" "是的，我曾經去過幾次。"

    "Have you been to that island?" "No, I haven't."
    "你去過那個島嗎？" "沒有，我沒去過。" 等等。

2. Can you suggest...? 你能向我推薦……嗎？例句：

    Can you suggest anything to eat?
    你能推薦什麼吃的東西嗎？

    Can you suggest anywhere to go?
    你能推薦什麼好玩的地方嗎？

    Can you suggest anything to buy?
    你能推薦什麼可買的東西嗎？

3. alone, by one's self, on one's own 都表示 "自己一個人"
    的意思。

    I often take a trip by myself.
    我經常自己一個人去旅行。

    He always finishes all the work on his own.
    他經常獨自一人完成所有工作。

2-15

服飾　Dress

對話 1

2-15-01.mp3

A: What do you think about my new dress? ↘
你覺得我的新衣服怎麼樣？

B: It really suits you. ↘ And your shoes are beautiful. ↘
非常適合你。你的鞋子也非常漂亮。

A: I feel very happy to hear what you said. ↘
非常高興聽到你這麼說。

對話 2

2-15-02.mp3

A: Do you like colourful clothing? ↗
你喜歡顏色艷麗的衣服嗎？

B: Yes. ↘ But I have to wear a uniform while working. ↘
是的。但是我上班得穿制服。

A: I love simple T-shirts and jeans. ↘
我喜歡簡單的 T 恤和牛仔褲。

B: You can try colourful clothing. ↘
你可以試試鮮艷的衣服。

對話 3

2-15-03.mp3

A: I bought a long skirt. ↘ How do you think of it? ↘
我買了一條長裙。你覺得怎麼樣？

B: Long skirts are my favourite. ↘ It's very nice! ↘
我最喜歡長裙了。非常漂亮！

A: Do you mean it? ↗ It's for you! ↘
你説的是真的嗎？是給你的！

B: I love it to death! ↘
我真是愛死它了！

對話 4

2-15-04.mp3

A: Are you fond of name brands? ↗
你喜歡名牌嗎？

B: Yes, I love buying name brands. ↘ LV is my favourite. ↘
是的，我喜歡買名牌。我最喜歡 LV。

A: Is it more practical? ↗
名牌更實用嗎？

B: I feel it makes me more confident. ↘
我覺得它能讓我更自信。

A: I can't tell the difference between the real and the fake LV
bags. ↘ So I've never had one. ↘
我分不清 LV 手袋的真品和仿冒品。所以我從來沒有買過。

More Sentences

2-15-05.mp3

你覺得……怎麼樣？

How do you think of ... ↘

Are you fond of... ↗

What's your opinion of ... ↘

我喜歡……

I love.... ↘

I like ...best ↘

My favourite ...is... ↘

2-16

網路　Internet

對話 1

A: What are you doing now? ↘
你在做什麼呢？

B: I am surfing on the Internet. ↘
我在上網。

A: Anything interesting? ↗
有什麼有趣的東西嗎？

B: I'm hooked on the Internet recently. ↘ There are large amounts
of information available on the Internet. ↘
我最近對網路有些上癮。網路上有太多信息了。

A: Could you recommend me a few good sites? ↗
能推薦給我幾個好的網站嗎？

B: What do you want to search? ↘
你想要查詢什麼？

A: I want to know the most popular movie these days. ↘
我想知道現在最流行的電影。

B: No problem. ↘
沒問題。

對話 2

2-16-02.mp3

A: Have you made Internet friends? ↗
你有網友嗎？

B: Yes, I have a lot of friends. ↘
是的，我有很多網友。

A: What kinds of people are they?
他們都是什麼樣的人？

B: All kinds. ↘ It's interesting to chat with a stranger online. ↘ And maybe some of them will become your friends. ↘
什麼樣的都有。在網上跟陌生人聊天很有意思。有些日後還會成為你的朋友。

A: Really? ↗ It's unbelievable. ↘
真的嗎？不可思議。

B: Now more and more people are turning to the Internet to find a mate. ↗
現在越來越多的人到網上尋找伴侶。

A: Not me. I don't believe in cyber-love.
我不會的。我不相信網上戀愛。

對話 3

2-16-03.mp3

A: How can I join your chat room? ↘
我怎樣才能加入聊天室呢？

B: It's easy. First, you have to create an ID.
很容易的。首先，你要註冊一個 ID 賬戶。

A: And then? ↗
然後呢？

B: Then you can chat with the people online. But don't get addicted to it. You may waste a lot of time.
然後你就可以和在線的人聊天了。不過，不要上癮啊。你會浪費太多時間的。

A: Don't worry about me. I am busy everyday. I'm curious about that. ↘
不必擔心。我每天都很忙的，不過好奇罷了。

B: That's fine.
那就好。

對話 4

2-16-04.mp3

A: What have you been doing recently, John? ↘
你最近忙什麼呢，約翰？

B: I've been chatting online a lot with friends. ↘
跟朋友在網上聊天呢。

A: Where do you go to chat? ↘
你去哪兒聊？

B: I usually use MSN. ↘ What about you? ↘
我通常用 MSN。你呢？

A: I've never chatted online before. ↘
我從不網上聊天。

B: What?! ↗ How is that possible? ↘ Why not? ↘
什麼？！怎麼可能？為什麼？

A: Well, I don't know how to use it. ↘
我不知道怎麼用。

B: Don't worry. ↘ Come over to mine, ↘ and I can show you
how to use it. ↘ I have wireless broadband. ↘ It's very
convenient. ↘
別着急。來我家吧，我教你怎麼用。我用無綫寬頻，非常方便。

A: Do you often download movies? ↗
你經常下載電影嗎？

B: Sure. ↘
當然啦。

對話 5

A: Have you ever bought anything online? ↘
你曾經在網上買東西嗎？

2-16-05.mp3

B: Sure. ↘ I often do shopping online. ↘ What about you? ↘
是啊。我經常在網上訂購。你呢？

A: I haven't tried shopping online. ↘
我從來沒有。

B: Why not? ↘ It's exciting to shop there. ↘
為什麼？網上買東西很讓人興奮。

A: Really? ↗ I'm afraid I will pay for nothing. ↘
是嗎？我擔心白白付款。

B: Most of the time it is safe. ↘ Anyway you'd better be careful. ↘
多數情況下是安全的。不過，不管怎麼說，還是小心為上。

對話 6

2-16-06.mp3

A: I want to buy some books online. ↘
Any books you want? ↗
我想在網上買幾本書。你有什麼想要的嗎？

B: Why not go to the bookstore? ↘
你為什麼不去書店呢？

A: They are cheaper online and it can save me a lot of time. ↘
網上買書便宜，而且節約很多時間。

B: Could you recommend some good sites? ↗
你能給我推薦幾個好的網站嗎？

A: Do you want to buy books, too? ↗
你也想買書嗎？

B: No, I want to buy some DVDs. ↘
不，我想買 DVD。

A: Okay. ↘
好的。

對話 7

2-16-07.mp3

A: I would like to try to make some orders with a shop online. ↘ Could you show me how to use it? ↗
我想要試試從網上商店訂貨。你能教我怎麼用嗎？

B: Sure. ↘ First you create an ID. ↘ Then choose from a variety of items. ↘ When you come to the last step for this deal, ↘ just click "go to the check out counter". ↘
當然可以。首先你註冊一個 ID 賬戶，然後選擇商品。到最後一步，點"去收銀台"就可以了。

A: How can I make the payment for the things? ↘
那我怎麼付款呢？

B: Many ways can be accepted online. ↘ Most of the time I choose cash on delivery as the way of payment. ↘ I think it's the best way. ↘
網上接受許多支付方式。我多數情況下選擇貨到付款。我認為那是最好的。

A: Thank you so much. ↘
非常感謝。

語法驛站

1. I'm hooked on the Internet recently. 我最近對網路有些上癮。Be hooked on 表示對……上癮。例如，He's hooked on heroin. 他吸食海洛英上了癮。如果是 Be hooked on sb. 則表示愛上某人。

2. Have you ever done...? 你曾經做過……嗎？這是一個表示現在完成時態的句子。現在完成時跨在兩個時間之上，一是過去，一是現在。動作發生在過去，但是對現在有影響，通常句子中沒有表示時間的詞或者短語。譬如：He has traveled over many lands. 他到過許多國家。Have you ever seen the sea? 你見過大海嗎？ She has had a good education. 她受過良好的教育。

3. It's exciting to shop there. 網上買東西很讓人興奮。Exciting 表示某事情或者某物讓人興奮。例如 That game is really exciting. 那個遊戲真讓人興奮。如果是某個人非常興奮，就要用 excited。例如 I'm excited at the program. 我對那個計劃感到很興奮。

約會　Dating

對話 1

A: Peter, you must come around sometime.
You have to check out my new stereo. ↘
彼得，你一定要找個時間過來。你得看看我新買的音響。

2-17-01.mp3

B: Sure. ↘ When's a good time for you? ↘
當然。你什麼時候方便？

A: Can you make it on Saturday? ↗
星期六可以嗎？

B: What time do you want me there? ↘
你希望我什麼時間到？

A: Any time would be fine. ↘
任何時間都可以。

B: All right. It's a date. ↘
好，就這麼定了。

對話 2

A: Jim, what are you doing now? ↘
占，你在做什麼呢？

2-17-02.mp3

B: I'm watching TV. ↘ What's up? ↘
我在看電視呢。什麼事？

A: Come and play tennis with me! ↘
來和我打網球吧。

B: But it's raining now. ↘
但是現在在下雨。

A: It's drizzle. ↘ Come on! ↘
不過是小雨。來吧！

B: Okay. ↘ Where to meet? ↘
好吧。在哪裏見面？

A: Let's meet at the gymnasium at 6. ↘
體育館，6 點鐘。

B: See you there. ↘
到時見。

對話 3

2-17-03.mp3

A: Are you busy this Saturday? ↗
這個週六你忙嗎？

B: I'm not sure. ↘ Why? ↘
我還不確定。怎麼？

A: Josh and I agreed to meet on the beach. ↘ If you were interested in swimming, ↘ we'd love to have you with us. ↘
Josh 和我約好去沙灘上玩。如果你對游泳感興趣，我們很希望你也能去。

B: I'd love to go out with you if I'm free. ↘ What time? ↘
我很願意跟你們去，如果我有時間的話。幾點鐘？

A: 10 in the morning. ↘
上午 10 點鐘。

B: That's great. ↘
好的。

語法驛站

1. When's a good time for you? 你什麼時間方便？這句話也可以這樣說：What time is good for you? 或者 When is good for you?

我們經常受到中文的影響，使用 convenient 這個詞，但實際上，外國人通常不說：What time is convenient for you?

2. Can you make it on Saturday? 星期六可以嗎？約定時間的時候，常常用到 make 這個詞。Make it 除了約定時間，還表示 "成功" 或者 "準時到達某個地方"。例如：

I made it to the airport just in time to catch my plane yesterday.
我昨天及時趕到飛機場搭上了我要乘坐的那班飛機。

Can you make a meeting at 8 a.m.?
你能趕上早上八點的會議嗎？

I'm not sure he'll make it. 我不確定他是否能夠成功。

英語會話
重練更易學

編著
Virginia Yannis

編輯
林榮生

講讀
Benjamin J. White, Kelly L. Roberts

美術設計
YU

排版
辛紅梅

出版者
萬里機構出版有限公司
香港鰂魚涌英皇道1065號東達中心1305室
電話：2564 7511
傳真：2565 5539
電郵：info@wanlibk.com
網址：http://www.wanlibk.com
　　　http://www.facebook.com/wanlibk

發行者
香港聯合書刊物流有限公司
香港新界大埔汀麗路 36 號
中華商務印刷大廈 3 字樓
電話：2150 2100
傳真：2407 3062
電郵：info@suplogistics.com.hk

承印者
中華商務彩色印刷有限公司
香港新界大埔汀麗路 36 號

出版日期
二零一八年十二月第一次印刷